Please return/renew this item by the last date shown.

North
Somerset
COUNCIL

How to make your felicity Wishes.

W I S H

With this book comes an extra special wish for you and your best friend.

Hold the book together at each end and both close your eyes.

Wriggle your noses and think of a number under ten.

Open your eyes, whisper the numbers you thought of to each other.

Add these numbers together. This is your

Magic Number

you

best friend

Place your little finger on the stars, and say your magic number out loud together. Now make your wish quietly to yourselves. And maybe, one day, your wish might just come true.   Love

felicity
x

For Millie 'Moo' Holt
with love from Auntie Emma

Emma Thomson's
felicity Wishes®

FELICITY WISHES
Felicity Wishes © 2000 Emma Thomson
Licensed by White Lion Publishing

Text and Illustrations © 2005 Emma Thomson

First published in Great Britain in 2005 by Hodder Children's Books

A Catalogue record for this book is available from the British Library

ISBN 0 340 90244 2

Printed and bound in Great Britain by Bookmarque Ltd, Croydon, Surrey

The paper and board used in this paperback by Hodder Children's Books are natural recyclable
products made from wood grown in sustainable forests. The manufacturing processes
conform to the environmental regulations of the country of origin.

Hodder Children's Books
A division of Hodder Headline Ltd, 338 Euston Road, London NW1 3BH

CONTENTS

Dreamy Drawings

It had been a very busy week for
Felicity Wishes. She was too tired to
go ice-skating with her best friends,
Holly, Polly and Daisy, so had decided
to stay at Sparkles, the café, and
order another frothy hot chocolate.

Felicity's week had been her most
hectic ever! On Monday she'd had
lunch-time flying club and cloud-
trekking after school. On Tuesday
she'd been to ballet class in the

evening. On Wednesday there was an acrobatics group rehearsal all day for the end-of-term show, and on Thursday she'd had double choir practice. She was utterly exhausted!

She had been idly flipping through magazines, toying with the idea of taking up a new hobby – something that required less physical effort than her other activities – when she'd fallen into a deep sleep.

"Felicity," whispered Gloria, the café owner, gently rocking her awake. "We're closing now."

Slowly Felicity pulled herself out of her dream.

"Wha... what? Where am I?" she stammered.

"You're here, in Sparkles, in Little Blossoming. Only I wish you weren't. I should have locked up ten minutes ago, but you looked like you needed a good rest so I left you for a little longer," said Gloria, glancing down at her watch. "Sorry, but I really have to dash now. I'm going to be late meeting a fairy decorator about giving this place a make-over."

"Sparkles? I'm not at home, in bed?" said Felicity, still a little bit befuddled.

"Yes, Sparkles café!" confirmed Gloria. "Look, I have to go. Fairy decorators are very hard to get hold of and this place is looking so shabby I can't afford to miss my appointment."

Gloria looked at her watch again. "I shouldn't really do this but I don't seem to have any choice. Can you lock up for me?" she said, handing Felicity a large bunch of keys. "If you could post them back through the letterbox when you've locked up, that would be brilliant. But, whatever you do, don't unlock the front door without double-locking the hallway door first. You'll set the alarm off."

Felicity rubbed her eyes sleepily, only half listening to what Gloria was saying.

"Promise?" called out Gloria, waiting for a response from Felicity.

"I promise," Felicity nodded, although she wasn't at all sure what she had just promised to do. And in a flutter Gloria was gone.

"Oh dear," said Felicity, stretching out her arms above her head. "Falling asleep in Sparkles, whatever next?

I really must try to slow down next week."

Felicity began to tidy up the area where she'd been sitting and as she picked up the magazines she remembered her last thoughts before she'd drifted off to sleep.

"A hobby that requires less effort..." she mumbled to herself as she flicked through the pages of a magazine again.

By the time Felicity had got to the end

of the article she knew exactly what she could do to relax. She would leave some of her other hobbies behind and take up painting instead!

Feeling refreshed and finally awake, Felicity picked up her bag and headed towards the hallway.

"Now what did Gloria say?" she asked herself out loud as she stood in the small area between the café and the front door. "Don't open the front door without double-locking the hallway door or I'll set the alarm off?"

Felicity was sure she'd remembered it right and carefully pulled the heavy door towards her.

Suddenly, deep in her tummy, Felicity had a feeling she'd forgotten something.

"My bag!" she spun around quickly to scan the floor.

"Oh!" she laughed to herself. "It's on my shoulder! Typical me!" And happily Felicity slammed the hallway door shut.

"Right then," she mumbled. Felicity always found it helped to talk to herself when completing a complicated task. "Double-lock the hallway door… before you open the front door."

Suddenly her face went pale.

"Keys!" she squealed. "Where are the keys?"

Frantically, Felicity emptied out the entire contents of her bag on to the hallway floor.

"NO!" she said to herself in disbelief. "I've left them on the table inside!"

* * *

Felicity had a dilemma. She couldn't go back and get the keys because the hallway door had locked automatically when she shut it. And she didn't dare open the front door because she would set off the alarm.

Felicity looked at her watch. It was ten past six. "No one is going to come to the café now until tomorrow morning," she sighed, putting her head in her hands. "I'm stuck here for the night. Unless..." she thought, "...I can call out to someone through the letterbox and get their attention!"

Felicity scrabbled over to the door and called out, "YOOOOOhoooooooo! Over here! Help!"

But even though the street outside was busy with shoppers and fairies returning home from school, Felicity's tiny cries went unheard.

"Well," she said, always eager to find a silver lining in any dark cloud. "I can use this time for some well-earned rest from my exhausting hobbies. With no phone and no one likely to call round I will be totally uninterrupted."

Suddenly Felicity had an amazing brainwave. "My mobile phone!" she squealed and rummaged frantically through all the mess on the floor before holding it up triumphantly. "With a dead battery!" she added, looking at the screen in disbelief and feeling her wings droop.

Suddenly overwhelmed, Felicity felt her eyes well up with tears. "I can't even wish my way out of here because it's against fairy law to make a wish for your own gain."

The hallway itself was dark. Used only as a passageway into the café, Felicity had hardly noticed its existence before. The shabby, neglected walls were bare and nothing stood in the entrance apart from a small table piled high with junk mail, and a tatty cardboard box with a dirty rag resting on top of it.

Ever resourceful, Felicity put her petticoat into her bag to make a cushion and began slowly reading her way through the pile of junk mail.

"Ouch!" she said out loud; she could feel pins and needles starting in her wings.

"I need to find something else to sit on," she whispered, glancing speculatively at her school books. But they looked just as hard as the floor.

Then, suddenly, she spied a cardboard box under the table.

"Perfect," she said as she reached over to pull it out. "Perhaps that will have something soft inside."

The box was much heavier than Felicity had imagined. Whatever was inside weighed a ton!

Sweeping off the dirty cloth that had been left on top of the box, Felicity eyed the seal. She knew it was naughty to open up without permission things that didn't belong to you. Then again, this wasn't the sort of situation where you could really ask for permission.

Felicity looked over both shoulders, even though she knew it was impossible that anyone would be there to see her naughty deed. Quickly she slid her wand under the seal, opened up the box and looked inside.

When she saw what the box contained, her heart leapt with delight. There was a silver lining to be found in the dark, cold 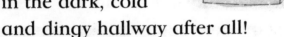 and dingy hallway after all!

* * *

Holly, Polly, and Daisy were concerned. The three fairies always met up before school for a gossip and a giggle, but today Felicity hadn't turned up.

They knew Felicity had been over-doing it lately with all the hobbies she was trying to squeeze into her already busy days.

"Felicity hasn't got any hobbies this morning, has she?" said Holly to the others.

"Not that I know of," said Daisy, looking out for Felicity approaching. "It's not like her to be this late without a reason."

"Unless she's overslept!" said Polly, who knew Felicity better than any of the fairies. "She was looking pretty sleepy in Sparkles when we left her last night!"

"That's true!" agreed Holly. "Let's fly to school via Felicity's house and check she's not still in bed."

With that, Felicity's three fairy friends were off.

* * *

But when they got to her house Felicity was nowhere to be seen.

"Oh, I do hope she's all right!" said Polly, becoming more worried by the minute.

"Her post is still on the mat," said Holly, peeping through the letterbox. "Felicity always opens her post first thing in the morning in case she's got a letter from Bea, her penfriend."

"There's still time to fly to Sparkles before assembly starts. Let's quickly go there and ask if they know where she went after we left her last night."

The fairies flew over to Sparkles much more quickly than any of them would usually fly that early in the morning!

"It's closed!" spied Holly, before they landed.

"Oh, but I can see the owner coming over the hill now," said Polly, pointing to the tiny figure in the distance.

"Morning!" called Holly, Polly and Daisy to Gloria.

"Morning!" she replied, cheerfully. "You must be desperate for hot chocolate if you can't even wait for me to open up!"

"Oh, it's not that!" explained Polly, flying beside her. "We've got to go to school, but we were worried about our friend, Felicity."

Gloria stopped flapping for a moment and frowned.

"You know, blonde hair, always wears pink, very friendly... She was with us yesterday afternoon," said Daisy desperately.

"Oh yes!" said Gloria. "She fell asleep in the café last night. Poor thing – she looked pooped! I left her with the keys to lock up as I had to dash to a meeting. I do hope she's remembered to post them back through the letterbox because I've only got one spare set."

"Do you know where she was going after she locked up?" asked Holly, impatiently.

"Bed, I expect!" joked Gloria as she put her key in the front door.

"That's strange," she said, confused. "I specifically asked Felicity to double-lock the door, but it has only been pulled closed."

Slowly the owner turned the key in the lock.

When the door opened, none of the fairies could believe their eyes.

"WOW!" they chorused, amazed by the brilliant mural of rolling hills and sparkling stars that met them.

"Wha... What? Where am I?" said Felicity, as she sat bolt upright from her sleep.

"What are you all doing in my bedroom?" she said, squinting at the four fairies who were looking at her, wide-eyed.

"We're not in your bedroom!" said Polly, softly. She pushed aside the paint pots that covered the floor and knelt down beside her friend. "You're in Sparkles hallway and it appears as though you've been here all night! And painting for most of it by the looks of things!"

"Why don't we all go inside for a nice mug of hot chocolate," suggested Gloria, who was having trouble believing her eyes, "and you can tell us all about it, Felicity. I'm sure Fairy Godmother won't mind you missing assembly just this once."

As the fairies filled up on hot chocolate and cookies, Felicity began to tell her story about opening the cardboard box in the hallway to discover lots of tiny tester pots of paint. Realising that she had a long night ahead of her, Felicity had decided to try out her new hobby.

"I don't know what time I finished," said Felicity, yawning. "I do feel a little sleepy but I really enjoyed it. Painting is actually very relaxing. I was thinking of taking it up as a hobby even before last night!"

"You definitely should!" said Gloria, delighted. "You clearly have a natural talent for it. The scene you painted is as beautiful as any professional decorator could have created, and an enormous improvement on the shabby walls that were there yesterday."

"So, you're not angry with me for opening your box and painting your walls without permission?" asked Felicity, tentatively.

"Not as long as you and your

friends promise to do the rest of the café!" said Gloria, giggling.

And everyone laughed, all except Felicity – who had fallen sound asleep again!

When you're looking for
an answer to a problem

magic will make the
answer find you

Happy Hobbies

Felicity Wishes had discovered a new talent – she was good at painting! Her discovery had happened quite by chance as a result of a rather unfortunate experience, when she'd become trapped overnight in the hallway of Sparkles café, with nothing to keep her amused but pots of paint!

Felicity had invited Holly, Polly and Daisy round to her house to try and introduce them to her new passion. Her friends were happy that Felicity had found a new hobby in which to pour all her boundless enthusiasm, but they weren't so keen to take it up themselves.

"Oh, come on!" encouraged Felicity. "Just give it a go. I know you'll enjoy it once you start. It's so much fun and very relaxing."

Holly looked fed up already. "I would much rather spend time on *my* favourite hobby – shopping!"

"I don't have natural talent like yours, Felicity," said Daisy, looking uncertainly at the pots of paint in front of them.

"None of us do," agreed Polly.

"It's not just talent," said Felicity. "It's mainly practice. My first paintings look terrible compared to the ones I can do now."

"I suppose you might be right," agreed Polly, reluctantly. "You don't achieve anything without hard work and none of us can expect to be any good at painting if we don't even give it a go."

Felicity grinned. She was enjoying her newly discovered hobby but would enjoy it even more if her friends liked it as well.

"Let's do something fun first!" said Felicity, pleased that she'd finally got her friends to pick up a paintbrush.

Very carefully, Felicity opened a

large pad of paper and tore off four
sheets.

"Right," she said, handing the
paper round. "Paint a head at the
top of the page. Any head will do. It
doesn't have to be good or true to life.
It can even be a flower head! Make
sure no one else sees what you've
done. When it's dry, fold it over and
pass the paper to the person on your
left."

Daisy giggled. "Any flower head?"
she asked, positioning her arm so
that none of her friends could see
what she'd chosen to paint.

Holly looked uninspired. "Can I
draw Fairy Godmother's head?"

"You can do any head at all!" said
Felicity, patiently.

When everyone had finished and
passed their folded paper on, Felicity
gave them the next instruction.

"Now paint a body. Any body. And

yes, Daisy, it can even be the body of a plant if you like!"

Holly, Polly and Daisy found Felicity's enthusiasm contagious and each of them spent ages getting the painting of their body just right.

"Fold over the paper, pass it on like before, and then paint some legs and feet," Felicity said next.

Giggling, the fairies pushed their bits of paper round and started painting again. When they'd finished they looked up at Felicity in anticipation.

"Now open it up!" said Felicity with a giggle.

Suddenly Felicity's kitchen erupted into loud laughter!

"Fairy Godmother's head with a flower stem body and legs like a duck!"

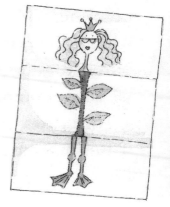

giggled Polly, hardly able to get the words out. "I've never seen anything so silly!"

"Well what about this then?" said Holly as she turned her picture around for everyone to see. "Floella's head with the body of a rabbit and the feet of a bird!"

Daisy nearly fell off her chair in hysterics!

"Let's do it again!" they all chorused.

* * *

For the next week there was no stopping the four fairy friends. Felicity's magical enthusiasm for painting had spread to all her friends with such sparkle, that there was barely a moment one of them was without a paintbrush!

They experimented by painting with opposite hands, and even with their feet.

They tried blindfolding each other
and drawing
from memory.

They even
tried backwards
painting in
the mirror,
underwater
painting in
the bath and
upside down painting while doing
handstands!

The more pictures they painted the
more confident they became.

* * *

As the fairies tumbled out of school
on Friday afternoon, Holly had a
suggestion for her friends.

"I know it's good fun experimenting,
but I think I've found the perfect
opportunity for us to try something a
little different." Holly rummaged
around in her bag and pulled out a

copy of 'Fairy Art' magazine. She opened it out to show her friends.

"What a great idea!" agreed Polly and Felicity enthusiastically.

"I'm not really very good at drawing faces," said Daisy. "Maybe if it was a competition for drawing flowers I'd be better."

"If we are going to become professional artists, we need to be able to draw fairies accurately," responded Holly. "It'll be fun drawing each other anyway."

"Don't worry, Daisy," said Felicity, quietly to her friend. "I'll help you practise painting fairies and you'll soon find 'real' painting just as fun as the silly stuff!"

✳ ✳ ✳

That weekend Felicity agreed to have

a portrait-painting day at her house.
Each of the fairy friends drew out a
name from Felicity's wish bag to
decide which friend they were going
to paint.

For the first part of the morning,
Felicity and Polly sat quietly while
Holly and Daisy sketched out their
portrait in pencil and then they
swapped places.

It wasn't until after lunch that they actually began to paint the portraits, which is when things started to go horribly wrong...

"I think it's best if no one shows anyone else their painting until it's finished," announced Felicity, who was worried that Holly would be upset if she saw how she looked in her painting.

"Yes," agreed Daisy, eagerly. Daisy wanted to be a Blossom Fairy when she graduated from the School of Nine Wishes and she had spent so much time painting the flowers in the background that she'd barely started painting Polly!

By the time the day drew to a close, it was clear that each of the fairies would need another day to complete their painting for the competition.

"Same time tomorrow?" called out Felicity to her friends as they flew their separate ways home, hiding their paintings under their wings.

"Yes," they all agreed, a little reluctantly.

* * *

That night Little Blossoming was in darkness except for four bedroom windows. The fairy friends were having trouble sleeping.

Unbeknown to each other, they had all pinned up their half-finished pictures on their bedroom walls and were anxiously trying to work out why it wasn't looking quite right.

"I think Polly's hair needs to be longer," mumbled Daisy, as she got out of bed to find a pencil.

"Holly's nose isn't as big as that," thought

Felicity to herself as she turned on her bedside light.

"I know Daisy is prettier than she looks here," mused Polly, squinting into the darkness.

"I think it will look better if I just rub out a few more of Felicity's freckles," thought Holly to herself as she began to alter her painting.

* * *

The next morning, when Holly, Polly and Daisy met up at Felicity's house, they were all yawning over their steaming cups of hot chocolate.

They had been up all night touching up, rubbing out and amending their portraits until finally sunshine had burst in through each of their curtains.

"Didn't you get much sleep last night?" said Felicity to Holly, noticing that her eyes seemed to be closing for longer than a blink.

"Um! Yes! Loads!" said Holly, telling a little white lie. She hadn't the heart to tell Felicity that her portrait wasn't looking as good as she'd hoped and couldn't bear to explain that she'd been up all night trying to make it look better.

"And you?" asked Holly. "You look a little sleepy yourself."

Felicity winced. She hated telling white lies. "Oh, I couldn't sleep because my mind was too alert after our cultural day of painting." How could she tell her friend she'd spent all night tinkering with her picture and now it was ruined?

"Well, we have a whole day of painting ahead of us and by the end of the day each of us will have a beautiful portrait to enter into the competition," Daisy said, trying to convince herself as much as the others.

"And one of us might even win first prize," said Polly, who imagined hers was the only bad painting amongst them.

But as the day went on, things just went from bad to worse. The more they rubbed out and painted over what they'd originally drawn the more awful the paintings looked.

"Whoever said painting was relaxing?" said Holly, who was getting very hot and bothered as her painting looked worse with every stroke of paint she added.

"How's my portrait looking?" Felicity asked Holly, bored of sitting still and anxious to have her turn at painting.

"It would look a lot better if you'd stop moving," said Holly, sharply.

Felicity had tried her best to sit as still as she possibly could, but her wings had started to ache and she was desperate for a Sparkle Bar.

"Holly's painting can't be going very well if she's blaming me for her mistakes," whispered Felicity to Daisy when Holly wasn't looking.

"How's your portrait of me going?" Daisy asked Polly, intrigued to find out if hers was going any better.

Polly looked uneasy.

"Hmm, maybe Felicity could be the judge of that," said Polly fretfully. "I'm thinking of starting again but I need a second opinion."

Felicity peeked tentatively around the corner of Polly's easel and had trouble stifling an enormous giggle. Polly's painting was almost as bad as her own. Daisy looked like she'd

Daisy
by
Polly

been pulled through a hedge backwards after running a marathon.

Felicity thought hard for a moment. Polly's enquiring eyes were looking at her intently.

"Oh, you don't need to start again," Felicity said encouragingly.

Polly looked relieved.

"All I'd say is that perhaps Daisy's hair could be calmed down a little," she said, unable to control a small giggle from escaping.

"You think my picture is horrible, don't you, Felicity?" said Polly, who wasn't taking the criticism well.

"No, not really," said Felicity, looking at Daisy and then back at the portrait.

"Then you're saying I'm having a bad hair day!" said Daisy, who had spent hours getting ready that morning.

"No!" protested Felicity.

"Then what?" asked Holly, who was itching to have a look at Polly's painting. "Is Polly's painting bad or is Daisy's hair-do awful in real life? It has to be one or the other."

Felicity gulped. Being the friendliest fairy in Little Blossoming, she always liked to be kind to everyone and she always tried her best never to hurt anyone's feelings, let alone her best friends'. But in this situation she didn't know what to do for the best.

"Neither!" Felicity burst out, feeling a white lie coming on. "My eyes are tired from all this painting, as I suspect yours are too." Her friends nodded in agreement.

"Why don't we take our easels out into the back garden to let our

45

paintings dry and, in the meantime, we can go to Sparkles for a milkshake break?"

"Good idea!" everyone agreed.

"Then, when we get back we can look at all of our paintings afresh," said Polly sensibly.

✳ ✳ ✳

Holly, Polly, Daisy and Felicity were all very relieved to have a break, and, secretly, none of them was really looking forward to returning.

After their third milkshake and fourth chocolate chip cookie, the fairies decided they couldn't put off the inevitable any longer.

"I guess we should be getting back," Felicity said reluctantly.

"It looks like it might rain," said Polly, glancing up at the dark clouds that had begun to gather in the sky.

"Oh no!" said Holly. "Our paintings! We left them outside to dry. If it rains our portraits will be ruined!"

"Oh goodness," said Felicity, watching the first specks of rain fall against the windowpane. "I can't find my shoe!" she said,  kicking it behind her bag. "I was playing with it under the table and now it's lost. Don't worry about my painting, you go on and save your own."

"I can't," exclaimed Holly. "I've misplaced my wand," she said, sitting on it. "And any fairy worth her wishes never goes anywhere without her wand."

Daisy and Polly looked at one another, then at Felicity and Holly, and giggled.

"Well we can't go," said Polly, speaking for both of them and watching with glee as the rain began to fall heavily outside, "because..."

She tried hard to think of an excuse.

"Because we all know our paintings will look a lot better after the rain than they did before!" said Holly, guessing correctly.

"Perhaps it might be better if we just stuck to the fun part of painting and left the serious portraits to the professionals," said Felicity, laughing.

And everyone agreed!

Magical Makeover

Felicity Wishes had been asked to do something rather exciting. It was a job that made her wings literally quiver with anticipation. She was honoured to have been asked and had hundreds of ideas but was worried she wouldn't be able to do it by herself.

So Felicity called an emergency meeting with her three fairy friends, Holly, Polly and Daisy, under the Large Oak Tree in the playing field at lunch-time. But she knew that enrolling their help wouldn't be easy...

"The owner of Sparkles café has asked me to give the interior a complete makeover!" Felicity announced proudly.

She had painted a beautiful mural in the entrance hall and now the owner wanted her to transform the entire café.

"Oh, how lovely!" said Polly. "We go there so often we barely notice how shabby it has started to look recently. But it hasn't been decorated for years."

Felicity nodded. "Apparently, last week a fairy complained about the wobbly leg of her chair. When the owner went to find her another one she discovered that all the chairs had wobbly legs!"

Daisy giggled. "I always thought wobbly chair legs were part of Sparkles' charm. Your milkshake keeps shaking even when you drink it!"

"So, what have you got planned, Felicity?" asked Polly.

"Well," said Felicity, tentatively. "I haven't actually said 'yes' yet as I'm not sure if I'll be able to cope with it all on my own," she said, looking hopefully at her friends.

Polly, Daisy and Holly all exchanged unhappy glances.

"You know we'd really like to help, Felicity," said Polly, glancing at the others who both nodded encouragingly. "But after the last painting project we did, none of us is very keen on using a paintbrush ever again."

Felicity loved painting and hoped her friends would too, but after a disastrous weekend of painting portraits, Felicity had learned a valuable lesson. Every fairy is different and there's a hobby to suit each one.

"I understand," said Felicity sadly.

"I'll let the owner know she'll have to find someone else for the job."

Holly, Polly and Daisy breathed a huge sigh of relief.

* * *

However, when Felicity arrived at Sparkles that night for a meeting with the owner, Gloria, things didn't go exactly to plan.

"Ah, Felicity!" said Gloria, giving her a big hug. "Have you had some ideas for our new-look café?"

"Oh yes!" said Felicity, sitting down at the table and pulling out her notebook. "Hundreds!"

Felicity opened the pages to show Gloria her drawings of colour schemes and themes that would give Sparkles the magical makeover it deserved.

"Oh I like the look of this!" said

Gloria, pointing to the pink and golden star combination that was secretly Felicity's favourite.

"I thought we could put stars on the ceiling, just like a night sky, and paint the walls in the pink glow of a sunset," said Felicity, clapping her hands together. "We could even use the same colours on the menus and the chair fabric so that it all ties in together."

"Oh yes!" said the owner, immediately visualising what Felicity imagined. "We could even make some new uniforms for the waitresses with tiny stars on the fabric."

"And they could have star notebooks, and stars on the end of their pencils too!" added Felicity.

"Yes, yes!" agreed Gloria, getting very excited. "Stars will be the perfect theme for a café called Sparkles! When can you start?"

"As soon as you want me to!" said Felicity, getting swept up in the enthusiasm. Then suddenly she remembered what her friends had said. "But…"

"But what?" asked Gloria.

Felicity looked awkward.

"Is there a problem?" said Gloria, hoping Felicity wasn't going to change her mind.

Felicity shifted from foot to foot, trying to work out what to do for the best. She really wanted to paint Sparkles, but surely she couldn't do it without her friends' help?

"I would really appreciate you doing this and as a thank-you present I would, of course, supply you with complimentary hot chocolates, ice cream and milkshakes for a whole year!" Gloria said, trying to persuade Felicity.

The temptation was too much.

Felicity had always had a sweet tooth and Gloria's offer was impossible to refuse. "I'll start today!" she said, already planning her first treat – a double-choc smoothie with milk chocolate sprinkles and a flurry of whipped cream.

* * *

Holly, Polly and Daisy hadn't seen Felicity for days when Daisy bumped into her in town, shopping.

"Oh hi, Daisy!" called Felicity from behind a stack of boxes.

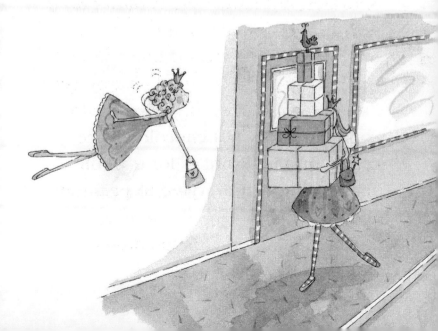

"I thought that was you!" giggled Daisy, flying up to peep over the top. "I recognised you by your stripy tights!"

Felicity put down all her boxes so she could see her friend properly.

"Felicity, you look exhausted. Whatever have you been up to?" said Daisy, concerned.

"Erm, well, I said yes to doing the makeover for the café in the end!" said Felicity, pointing to the large sign that hung outside the café.

Closed for
Magical Makeover
Grand re-opening on Saturday at 11a.m.

"I have been decorating the place before and after school and during lunch-time too," said Felicity, sitting down on her box to have a rest. "I'm exhausted but it will be worth it."

"That's why we haven't seen you for ages," said Daisy.

"Actually," continued Felicity, trying to catch her breath. "You could help me!"

Daisy looked awkward. "I thought we already agreed, Felicity, that everyone has their favourite hobby and mine is most definitely not painting! I'm just no good at it."

"No!" said Felicity. "I don't mean help with the painting, but I could do with a hand carrying these boxes inside. Now I've put them down I'm not sure I can pick them all back up again!"

"Oh!" Daisy gasped. "Yes, of course I will."

Daisy and Felicity piled into the café with arms full of cardboard boxes.

"Wow!" said Daisy, when she saw

what Felicity had already done. "It looks like a different place."

Most of the walls had been stripped of their old wallpaper, the carpets had been taken up, the furniture was neatly stacked in a pile to one side and on the far wall Felicity had painted a beautiful sunset mural.

"Wow! It's so good, it almost looks real!" said Daisy, genuinely impressed.

"Thanks," said Felicity, "but I can't help thinking it's missing something so I brought these." Felicity opened up one of the boxes to reveal hundreds of pink flowers in every shape, size and shade imaginable.

"Oh, they're so beautiful!" Daisy exclaimed. She wanted to be a Blossom Fairy one day and was very green-fingered.

"I was going to stick them on with this," said Felicity, pulling out an enormous tube of industrial glue.

Daisy winced. She loved flowers and talked to her plants daily to make them grow. Sticking such beautiful blooms to a wall with such irreverence made her cringe.

"Why don't you press them first and then attach each one with a tiny sprinkling of sparkledust?" she suggested to Felicity. "They'll keep their colour much better that way."

Felicity looked thoughtful. "I'd like to, but I just don't have time. I still have so many other jobs to do and I promised Gloria I would be finished by Saturday for the grand opening."

"I'll help!" offered Daisy, who still couldn't take her eyes off the wonderful flowers.

"But I thought you didn't want to help?" said Felicity, confused.

"That was painting. Pressing flowers is another matter entirely. It's one of my favourite hobbies and

I'd enjoy every moment."

Felicity was
overjoyed, and
as Daisy set
to work,
Felicity
dashed off
back into town
to complete the next task on her list.

* * *

The fabric shop in Little Blossoming
was full from floor to ceiling with
every kind of material a fairy could
wish for – glittery silks, twinkly netting
and the softest satins you could ever
imagine.

"Can I help?" asked the fairy
assistant politely.

"Yes, please," said Felicity. "I'd like
some pink fabric with gold stars that
can be used for covering chairs and
sofas... and for making dresses," she
added, remembering Gloria's

suggestion about the waitresses' uniforms.

The assistant hurried off to see if they stocked anything suitable.

"Are you making dresses?" said a voice from behind a large rack of cotton reels.

"Holly!" said Felicity surprised. "What are you doing here?"

"I've been invited to the grand opening of Sparkles on Saturday but I've nothing to wear! I've tried every dress in Little Blossoming but I can't find one I like. So I thought I'd look in here to see if there were any inspirational dress patterns."

"Holly, you have a wardrobe full of amazing dresses. Surely you don't need another one?" said Felicity.

"I suppose I don't *need* one." admitted Holly. "What I need is an excuse to create something original and exciting to wear. I've looked through all of these books but nothing really excites me."

Holly was the fairy fashion queen of the School of Nine Wishes and loved to be the first to discover a new trend, but some trends only lasted a week or two, so Holly's wardrobe was crammed with outfits that she had only worn once!

"I love the sound of the material you've chosen though," continued Holly. "I don't suppose you want help making your dress?"

Felicity's crown nearly pinged off her head with excitement, but then she remembered that Holly didn't want to help out in Sparkles.

"Well, actually it's not one dress, it's four!"

Holly stared blankly at Felicity.

"I decided to do the Sparkles makeover after all," said Felicity, looking sheepish. "So I don't suppose…"

"I'd love to!" said Holly, getting quite excited at the prospect. "You know fashion is one of my favourite pastimes, there's nothing I'd enjoy more!"

So Felicity left Holly happily buying buttons and zips for the dresses and returned to the café with the fabric for the furniture.

When she opened the door, Felicity could hardly believe her eyes. Daisy had transformed the mural that Felicity had carefully painted on the back wall into a floral feast, and now she was making co-ordinating menu cards for each table.

"I hope you don't mind," she said, seeing Felicity's shocked expression. "But there were so many star flowers left over, it seemed a shame to waste them. I was even thinking that I could make some flowery covers for the waitresses' notebooks too."

"Lovely!" said Felicity, barely able to contain her joy. She got out her list of things to do and put a big tick by the things she and her friends had already done.

To do:
Cover chairs/sofas
Paint walls ✓
Paint mural ✓
Stick flowers ✓
Make menu cards ✓
Make uniforms ✓
Take up carpet ✓
Clean floor ✓
Book event for opening night

* * *

"Almost everything that's on my to-do list is done!" squealed Felicity with delight. "I've just got to cover these sofas and chairs

66

and the makeover will be complete."

Felicity walked over to the mountain of chairs and sofas that awaited her transformation. She gulped at the prospect of carrying them all the way back across the room. Her wings were still hurting from moving them earlier.

"Hello?" called someone through the letterbox. "Can I come in? It's me, Polly!"

"Polly!" said Felicity, opening the door to her friend. "What a nice surprise!"

"I phoned Holly earlier to ask if she wanted to go shopping but she was having too much fun sewing dresses! I realised I must be missing out on something really exciting if Holly was turning down a shopping trip, so here I am!"

"Come in, come in!" said Felicity. "The more the merrier!"

"My gym is closed today while they fit some new equipment," said Polly disappointedly, "and there's no other hobby I really feel like doing today. I had hoped to improve my muscle tone ready for the pillow lifting trials when we go back to school."

Polly wanted to be a Tooth Fairy when she graduated from the School of Nine Wishes and spent every spare moment preparing for her future career.

"Are there any other ways of increasing your strength other than going to the gym?" asked Felicity, suddenly having an idea. "You could lift up these sofas and chairs while I cover them, if you want?"

"Are you sure?" asked Polly. "I wouldn't want to get in your way."

"You wouldn't," insisted Felicity. "Really, you'd be helping me enormously."

And with that the two fairy friends set to work.

By lunch-time on Friday, the Sparkles café makeover was complete. Each of the fairy friends had used their favourite hobbies to achieve miraculous results.

"Wonderful, wonderful!" said Gloria, when she arrived to inspect the finished effect. "A truly amazing transformation!"

Holly, Polly, Daisy and Felicity grinned proudly.

"I am so looking forward to the grand opening tomorrow. What entertainment did you decide on in the end?" asked Gloria, still admiring the fairy friends' handiwork.

Suddenly, Felicity went pale and then quickly consulted her to-do list. She'd been so happy that all of her

friends had helped her that she'd totally forgotten to book the entertainment for the opening!

"Erm, erm, if you give me two minutes I'll just consult my team," said Felicity, dragging her friends

into a corner of the room. After a lot of whispering, she turned back to Gloria. "I am happy to say that we would be delighted to open the café tomorrow with an extra-special star dance that we all learnt at ballet class."

Gloria looked unsure. "I don't mean to sound rude, but I was hoping for something a little more professional. Do you think it will be good enough to do this incredible transformation justice?"

"Absolutely!" said Felicity, confidently. "Ballet is our favourite hobby – or, should I say, it was until we discovered the fun of makeovers!"

If you enjoyed this book, why not try another of these fantastic story collections?

Clutter Clean-out

Designer Drama

Newspaper Nerves

Star Surprise

Enchanted Escape

Friends Forever

Sensational Secrets

Whispering Wishes

Happy Hobbies

Party Pickle

Wand Wishes

Christmas Calamity

Dancing Dreams

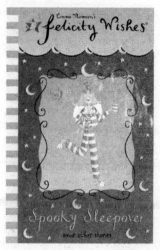

Spooky Sleepover

Fashion Fiasco

Also available in the Felicity Wishes range:

Felicity Wishes: Secrets and Surprises

Felicity Wishes is planning her birthday party but it seems none of her friends can come. Will Felicity end up celebrating her birthday alone?

Felicity Wishes: Snowflakes and Sparkledust

It is time for spring to arrive in Little Blossoming but there is a problem and winter is staying put. Can Felicity Wishes get the seasons back on track?

Felicity Wishes: Mix-ups and Magic

Felicity Wishes fairy friends are terribly down in the dumps. Without realising it, Felicity makes a wish for each of her unhappy friends, but Felicity's wishes are a little mixed-up...

Felicity Wishes: Friendship and Fairyschool

It is nearly the end of school for Felicity Wishes and all her friends know exactly what kind of fairies they want to be – but poor Felicity does not have a clue!

The World of Felicity Wishes

Felicity Wishes' world is full of wonderful, sparkly things. Friends that make her giggle, fashion that makes her tingle and a million other yummy things that she can't wait to share with you.

In this stunning novelty book, you can discover Felicity's secret hiding places, meet her best friends and learn the Fairy Dance routine. You can also find out what type of fairy you could be!